Does the lost EYE OF THE FATES still exist?

51

What strange powers does ~~it~~ *51* possess?
What are the sinister forces that will stop at nothing to keep you from finding it?

These and other questions will be answered as you and Indiana Jones™ risk your lives on your ~~perilous~~ quest.

You will have to make many ~~last-minute~~ decisions. Just follow the directions at the bottom of each page.

Make the right choices and you could both end up being heroes.

But let this be a warning: The wrong decision could mean your doom!

Good luck on your quest for the Eye of the Fates. You'll need it!

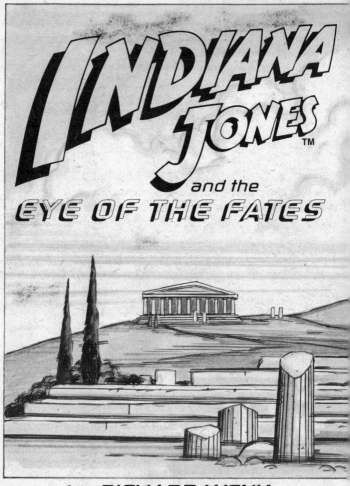

INDIANA JONES

JONES ™

and the

EYE OF THE FATES

by RICHARD WENK

Illustrated by DAVID B. MATTINGLY

SPHERE BOOKS LIMITED
London and Sydney

First published in Great Britain by
Sphere Books Ltd 1984
30–32 Gray's Inn Road, London WC1X 8JL
Copyright © 1984 Lucasfilm Ltd. (LFL)
TM: 'Find Your Fate' is a Trademark of Random House,
    Inc.
    'Indiana Jones' is a Trademark of Lucasfilm Ltd.
Used under authorisation.
This edition published by arrangement with Ballantine Books,
A Division of Random House, Inc.

Designed by Gene Siegel

Cover and interior art by David B. Mattingly

For Doug McKeown, with heartfelt thanks

TRADE
MARK

This book is sold subject to the condition that
it shall not, by way of trade or otherwise, be lent,
re-sold, hired out or otherwise circulated without
the publisher's prior consent in any form of
binding or cover other than that in which it is
published and without a similar condition
including this condition being imposed on the
subsequent purchaser.

Printed and bound in Great Britain by
Cox & Wyman Ltd, Reading

INDIANA JONES™
and the
EYE OF THE FATES

Find Your Fate™ Adventure #4

**Off the coast of Greece
August 1937**

"Well, Indiana Jones?" your father asks. "What have you got?"

"Only the find of the century!" says Indy Jones, grinning widely as he pulls off his diving suit.

The famous archeologist has just climbed back on board your father's salvage boat. He has been exploring a sunken wreck, over five thousand years old. Your father, the curator of an American museum, is hoping to prove that the wreck is a ship that belonged to Perseus, the legendary Greek hero.

"The shield of Perseus," announces Indy, holding up a broken disk hammered out of pure gold. Greek sailors and news reporters crowd around.

"It's the find of the century, all right," says your father, putting on his glasses. "It's also the *mystery* of the century."

You can see some fragments of a message etched in Greek on the back of the shield. Indy tells you he thinks these are clues to the location of one of the wonders of the ancient world: the lost Eye of the Fates!

....

Turn to page 2.

Indy explains that, according to one legend, the Fates were three blind old women who once lived in the Far East. They shared among them one magic crystal Eye, fashioned by the Greek gods. Looking through it, they were able to see the fates of everyone and everything in the world.

"So," Indy concludes, "it's said that whoever possesses the Eye has the power to see the future—and to change it."

One of the crew, a Greek sailor named Costas, translates the ancient message on the shield:

I, PERSEUS THE GREEK, (Costas reads) STOLE THE EYE FROM THE THREE WOMEN OF HOKK—

Here the line breaks off. Costas reads the next line:

—RETURNED IT TO THE GODS

"Jones," says your father, "can you follow these clues? Think you can find the Eye of the Fates?"

"If it still exists," says Indy, "I'll find it! Just don't let this story get out. The power of the Eye may just be a myth, but I wouldn't take any chances. If it should get into the wrong hands—"

Holy smoke! The boat is full of reporters! And you just remembered that there's a radio in the cabin! The story *will* get out!

Turn to page 3.

By the time you run to the cabin, it is too late. The reporters have radioed the story. Now the whole world will know about the clues on the shield.

Indy is very worried. He takes you and your father aside.

"We'll have to work fast," he says, studying the mysterious message. "The way I figure it, the letters HOKK could mean 'Hokkaido,' which is in northern Japan. Maybe the Eye is hidden there."

"Wait a minute," you say. "If Perseus returned it to the gods, maybe it's buried right here in Greece. Wasn't Mount Olympus supposed to be the home of the gods?"

"Good thinking, kid," says Indy. "You're going to be a big help." He turns to your father. "Smart kid you've got here."

Your father has to stay on board to oversee the salvage operation. But you can go along with Indy!

The question is, should you take another boat and sail to Mount Olympus? Or should you fly to Japan?

....

If you decide Japan's the best bet, turn to page 9.

If you'd rather sail to Mount Olympus, turn to page 19.

3

Wide-eyed, the chief priest takes the shield of Perseus from Indy and bows to it. All the other worshippers come up and do the same. Then they all bow down to you!

"Nice work, kid," whispers Indy.

"The shield!" you gasp. "They must think we're gods, or something!"

Everyone in the cave starts to chant in unison. Now the words sound familiar.

"They're chanting the inscription on the shield," Indy tells you.

"I wonder if they know where the Eye of the Fates is," you say. You gesture at the shield and shrug your shoulders, and everyone seems to understand you. They begin to whisper with excitement. Then they nod their heads and smile.

From the altar the old priest removes a scroll, cracked and brown with age. He beckons you and Indy to follow the whole congregation through a concealed passageway in the wall.

"When did you take up sign language?" Indy asks.

You shrug your shoulders.

Indy laughs. "Come on," he says. "We might as well follow them up these steps. Maybe they lead to the Eye!"

Turn to page 24.

The horses can't follow you up the rocky hillside. You and Indy duck into the first cave you come to.

"If they dismount and follow us," says Indy, "we're goners. Hurry!"

You run deeper and deeper into the dark cave. The light grows dim. You run past a tunnel forking off to the left.

Pretty soon the cave narrows and the walls close in on you.

"We can't keep going this way," you say. "There's no room. And almost no air."

"It's not easy on the eyesight, either," says Indy, squinting. "Well, what do we do? Go back?"

"Maybe this cave opens out up ahead," you say uncertainly. "We could keep going and see. But there was a tunnel back there. It might lead to the other side of the island."

....

If you think it's safer to go back, turn to page 110.

If you decide to continue, turn to page 45.

5

Suddenly you can breathe again. There is a bright light. You are walking with Indy in a wide, level cavern. The light comes from a torch held by a hunched old peasant woman who walks ahead of you.

For some reason, you don't question this strange turn of events.

"Try to hold out a little longer," says Indy's echoing voice. "She seems to know the way out."

The toothless old woman guides you into a spectacular chamber. The walls are made of silver and gold. They are studded with thousands of oval-shaped enamel tiles.

Each tile is painted to look like a human

eye. You feel like you are being stared at from all over.

Black velvet drapes are suspended from the ceiling. Resting against one wall are two oblong marble cases.

"I hate to say it," says Indy, "but those things look like coffins."

Without warning, the old hag begins to wail and keen in a high-pitched voice. Then she breaks off in choking sobs.

You and Indy look at each other in alarm. What's wrong with her?

Turn to page 66.

You are in a deep chasm, surrounded on all sides by sheer cliffs. Not even a foothold. There is no way out!

"Now what?" you ask wearily. You hear a strange buzzing in your head.

"I would say it's time for a rest," says Indy, staring straight ahead, "but if I'm seeing what I think I'm seeing, we're gonna have to act fast."

In the middle of the chasm is a mammoth old olive tree, growing in the sunlight between the cliffs. But this is no ordinary tree. It is golden yellow. And it's moving! Suddenly you realize what the strange buzzing sound is. The ancient tree is completely covered with huge yellow bees!

"I hate bees!" you yell.

"Quiet!" says Indy. "They'll attack!"

But it's too late. The millions of bees have swarmed off the tree and are heading straight for you!

Turn to page 56.

You and Indy are the only passengers on board the chartered plane to Japan. To pass the time, you daydream about the adventures that lie ahead.

Suddenly Indy jumps up and rushes to the window.

"There's something funny going on," he says suspiciously. "We should be flying due east."

"So what?" you say, still half dreaming.

Indy frowns. "So which way is the sun?" he asks.

"Out the right-hand window," you answer.

The right-hand window! You realize what Indy is saying. "Hey!" you shout. "That means we're flying south!"

"Right," snaps Indy, running to the front of the plane. "Hey, you! Pilot! Turn this crate around!"

Your Japanese pilot slides back a partition. He is training a pistol on you!

"Get down, kid!" shouts Indy, pulling out his own gun. Suddenly the air is filled with gunshots. The pilot closes his partition. You're being skyjacked!

Should you try to overcome the pilot and fly the plane yourselves? Or should you use your parachutes to bail out?

....

If you decide to bail out, turn to page 10.

If you decide to disarm the pilot, turn to page 31.

Hiding behind a seat, you quickly strap on your parachutes.

"Don't forget," Indy whispers to you. "As soon as we get the door open, jump. Then count to ten and pull your ripcord."

But the pilot has seen what you're up to. He begins to fire again through the partition. He's really trying to kill you!

Indy unbelts the back of the seat and holds it up as the two of you run to the door. Bullets rip into the upholstery.

"Word sure got around fast," says Indy, pulling open the door. "I wonder how many people will try to stop us from getting the Eye. Now jump!"

As you plummet down in freefall, you can see the blue Aegean Sea far below, and the west coast of Crete.

On the count of ten, you pull your cord.

Nothing happens! You are still falling. Your parachute has failed.

You close your eyes and wait for the end.

Turn to page 13.

At first, you and Indy slip and slide down the inclined passage, ducking your heads to avoid the jagged rocks. The roar of the water below gets louder. The passage gets steeper and more slippery.

All at once, it feels like you're sliding down a greased chute. You pick up speed.

"Lie on your back!" shouts Indy as he shoots feet first ahead of you down the tunnel.

You must be doing fifty miles an hour.

"Just like the funhouse," you yell happily.

"I'm glad *you're* having fun!" Indy yells back.

You both land feet first with a splash in the underground river. A strong current carries you rapidly away.

"Don't try to fight it!" cries Indy. "Just go with it!"

Above you, rushing by, you can see the cavern ceiling, lit by the faint glow of luminous fungi. Hundreds of stalactites zip by, like multicolored Christmas tree ornaments.

"Look out!" Indy warns.

Dead ahead is a wall of rock! The river rushes beneath it. If you get swept under, you won't be able to come up for air!

Turn to page 74.

Suddenly a strong arm grabs you in midair. Indy waited just long enough to reach you before pulling his cord. There is a rough lurch as his chute opens. You open your eyes.

With a gentle swinging motion, both of you float down toward the sandy beach and land with a splash in the surf.

"Thanks. That was close," you say, standing in the waves.

"Yeah, too close," says Indy, taking off his harness. "It's a good thing my chute worked."

You follow Indy up the beach. There should be a fishing village nearby. You've got to tell the police about that murderous pilot.

"Indy, look!" you shout. Coming right for you is an angry band of Cretan locals on horseback.

"I didn't see a 'No Trespassing' sign," says Indy, "but these people pull their knives first and ask questions later. We've got to get out of here."

But which way? There are hills at the edge of the beach, and they're studded with caves. That's one way. And there is a tiny islet about a hundred yards off shore. That's another way.

If you decide to run to the caves, turn to page 5.

If you decide to swim to the islet, turn to page 22.

You slowly open your eyes. You can see! You are lying in a hospital bed. Standing next to you is your father. Across the room is Indiana Jones.

"Glad to see you come around, kid," Indy says. "We were worried."

"You were in a coma," your father explains. "You passed out from lack of oxygen in that cave. Jones brought you to the hospital here in Athens. You've been here for four days."

And guess what? While you were dreaming away, Indy flew to Japan alone. He found the Eye of the Fates, a magnificent jewel, the "find of the century."

And you missed the whole thing.

"When's your next adventure?" you ask Indy. "I still have two weeks left before my summer vacation comes to—"

THE END

The Minotaur lowers its head and lunges right at you. But Indy acts fast. He dives and tackles you just as the monster rushes past.

It crashes into the wall.

But that doesn't stop it. With great agility, it spins and lunges again. This time at Indy. He will be gored to death by those sharp horns!

Now it is your turn to act fast.

You throw yourself on your knees in front of its charging legs, just before it gets to Indy.

The heavy beast topples to the dirt. Indy brings the shield of Perseus down on its head with a crash.

It has no effect! This thing is invulnerable!

Without so much as a grunt of pain, the Minotaur grabs Indy's leg and twists violently. Indy is thrown to the floor.

There is only one chance you can think of to stop it. You bite its leg with all your strength.

Howling in pain, it scrambles up and starts swinging at you like a boxer. As you duck the blows, Indy pulls out his pistol and fires.

The bullet bounces off the monster's neck. Can nothing kill this thing?

Turn to page 70.

15

Almost too late, you understand what Indy has done.

He has tossed the Eye to you! You catch it automatically. At the same time, Indy kicks the oil lamp and smashes it. The three of you are plunged into darkness.

"Run!" shouts Indy. "Run for the rope ladder!"

You hear the Nazi's gun firing in the dark. But you follow Indy's orders and run right around the blasting gun and out the open door.

You are almost at the edge of the cliff, and Indy is right behind you.

"He's gaining on us," says Indy. "Hurry!"

You uncoil the rope ladder and send it over the edge. You and Indy climb down much faster than you climbed up. You are clutching the Eye of the Fates in your hand.

A gun blast from above sends a bullet whizzing past your head. Then you hear another sound.

Click! Click!

The Nazi is out of ammunition. Maybe you'll make it after all. But you happen to glance into the Eye.

"Indy, look!" you cry.

You can see what the Nazi is doing high above you. He is cutting the rope ladder!

Turn to page 119.

This was a bad decision.

Indy was right. While you cling to the wildly shifting rock, you hear a great rumbling roar from the very center of the mountain.

You'd better get used to the water. You will be spending a long time in it.

Still holding on, you are dragged by tons of rock into the rushing whirlpool, down to a deep sea grave.

THE END

It is a beautiful, clear day on the Aegean Sea. The great Perseus once sailed these waters thousands of years ago. And now here you are, on an adventure with a modern-day hero!

"Look!" you cry, pointing off the port bow. "There's Mount Olympus."

The ancient home of the gods towers majestically over the sunny coast.

"I think we're almost to port," says Indy, holding his hat against the wind. "Hey, Costas!"

The Greek sailor has agreed to be your guide. Now he comes over to Indy.

"Yes," he says. "That is the port dead ahead."

BOOM!

The three of you are thrown to the deck by the force of a violent explosion!

There is so much smoke, it is hard to assess the damage. But the boat seems to be listing severely.

If an enemy planted one bomb, he might have planted two. At any moment the whole boat could blow up.

Should you try to take it into port for repairs, or should you abandon ship? There's not much time to decide.

If you decide to abandon ship, turn to page 58.

If you decide to try and save the boat, turn to page 35.

19

The chanting grows louder as the mass of robed figures stretch their arms out toward the sunlight.

"It must be some ancient dialect!" shouts Indy above the noise. "I can't understand any of the words."

"It's Greek to me," you shout back jokingly.

But you have made a mistake. Just as you shout, the chanting stops. Everyone has heard you.

One by one the pale faces turn to you.

A tall man with a beard takes a step forward. He seems to be the chief priest.

"Bottas daklo," he growls.

They all begin to pull out short, razor-sharp knives. Then they move toward you.

"This is not a welcoming party," says Indy. "If we run for it now, we might stand a chance."

"Yeah, but if they catch us," you say, "they might cut us to pieces! Maybe we should just stand still and show them we mean no harm."

What should you do?

If you decide to run, turn to page 27.
If you decide to stand still, turn to page 92.

20

"Wh-what is *that*?" you ask, your voice shaking.

"I'm not sure I want to find out," says Indy. "Let's get out of here. Look what I found."

He's discovered a rough doorway cut into the wall. You push your way through, into a small room lit by a torch lying on the dirt floor. In the middle of the room is a pile of earth and a deep hole.

"Somebody's just been here," says Indy, "and I'll bet I know why."

There is something behind you! You spin around to face the most frightening creature you have ever seen.

It is a huge black bull, about six feet tall, with sharp, curving horns. But it has the body of a man! It is the legendary monster of the labyrinth—the Minotaur!

"I don't believe this," whispers Indy.

Rumbling and snorting, the great monster stamps the ground, as if pawing at it.

"I don't know about mythical minotaurs," says Indy, "but in bull language, that means we're in for it."

Turn to page 15.

It is a longer swim than you thought. Just when you can keep afloat no longer, Indy is dragging you onto the islet.

It seems to be just a big rock, about twenty feet around and eight feet high.

Back on shore, the horsemen have given up and ridden away. You turn to Indy. You want to know if it's safe to swim back.

"Hey," he says, pointing into the clear water, "look. We're sitting on the peak of an undersea mountain!"

Sure enough, you can clearly see the rocky surface sloping down into the darkness.

Just then the sea goes wild. Like a sudden storm, waves lash up at you, covering the islet and washing over it.

"Hang on!" shouts Indy. *"Earthquake!"*

The whole peak is shaking violently. The waves crash over you and you struggle to keep your hold. You are afraid the sea will tear you loose.

"This whole mountain may sink beneath us!" shouts Indy. "We could be sucked down in the undertow! Let's swim for shore!"

He dives into the huge waves and heads for Crete.

If you are brave enough to follow, turn to page 88.

If you'd rather stick to the rock, turn to page 18.

Just as you are about to ask Indy what to do next, he puts his finger to his lips.

"Listen!" he whispers. "We have to find out as much as we can."

Out of sight above, you hear voices murmuring. Who is talking? You can't understand the words.

A moment later there is a scuffling sound and the rustling of bushes. You hear a confusion of shouting voices. Someone is being chased!

Then there is silence.

"I thought so," says Indy. "Mishi is not an enemy. He was forced into this."

"How do you know?" you ask.

"I'll tell you later," he replies. "But first we have to get out of here."

If you try to climb back up, there is a chance that some of the masked men are waiting to kill you. If you start searching for another way out, you might get lost in the underground dig.

What should you do?

If you decide to climb out, turn to page 62.
If you decide to search, turn to page 96.

The stone stairway leads all the way to the top of the mountain. You emerge into brilliant sunlight. Below lies the coast of Crete and the sky-blue waters of the Aegean Sea.

The priest opens the scroll. His eyes are squinted closed, unaccustomed as he is to the bright sun. But you and Indy see at once what's on the scroll.

"A picture of the Eye of the Fates!" says Indy. "And the drawing is signed by Perseus."

He starts looking around for the Eye. But the sun worshippers, shielding their eyes, chatter and point to the sky.

Suddenly you understand.

"Indy, um...Indy," you say, tapping him on the shoulder. "I hate to disappoint you, but remember the myth? The Eye was made by the gods. It could see the fates of everyone and everything in the world. And the three women were blind without it."

"So?" says Indy.

"So," you say with a sigh, "guess what the Eye was, and still is."

You cover your eyes like the sun worshippers and slowly point up.

The Eye of the Fates is—the sun!

THE END

He hands you two stones and crawls slowly backward.

"When I say 'go,' strike the flint," he tells you. "And then run like your life depends on it—because it does!"

Your hands shaking, you hold the two rocks over the powdery fuse. You'll only get one chance. One of the bees flies down close to your ear. But you don't dare move.

You hear Indy shout "Go!" and you strike the flint.

The fuse is lit!

You run like mad back to the hole in the rock and dive headfirst into the underground river.

Some of the bees have taken off after you. But it is too late for the rest.

As you and Indy dunk your heads in the water, you hear a small explosion and a *whoosh*!

The tree is in flames. Burning bees fall by the thousands. The rest escape, buzzing furiously. They fly off in confusion, over the cliffs and out of the chasm.

The burning tree sends smoke billowing high up into the blue sky. Indy makes you wait almost an hour before he says it is safe to come out.

When you do, you realize that the bees may be gone, but you are still trapped!

....

Turn to page 38.

Suddenly you point up to the chink in the roof, where the sunlight streams in, and yell, "Look out!"

As the evil-looking sun worshippers turn sharply around to see what you're pointing at, you say to Indy:

"That's our headstart. Let's move!"

The two of you take off as fast as you can, back down the cave tunnel. Behind you, shouting in anger, the robed figures begin the chase.

"In here!" says Indy. He has ducked into a shallow passageway. Just in time! The ghostly people, their knives flashing, run right past into the dark. Soon they have disappeared down the tunnel.

"I hear water running," you say, puzzled.

"It's coming from over there," says Indy, crossing the cave. There you find two small tunnels, one sloping up, the other down.

"There must be an underground river or spring down this tunnel," you say.

"But the one slanting up," says Indy, "might come out on top of the island. We could get away."

The waterway could lead to the harbor. It's a tough decision. But you hear the sun worshippers coming back! You have to decide *now*!

....

If you choose the "up" tunnel, turn to page 55.

If you choose the "down" one, turn to page 12.

You are completely surrounded by the masked thugs. There are about twenty of them, each holding a rifle trained on you and Indy.

"Welcome, Jones," murmurs a quiet voice. "Welcome."

A tall, dark man with a thin mustache steps forward. He is not wearing a mask. Indy recognizes him.

"Claude Belloq!" he says with a gasp. "So you're behind this."

"Of course," replies Belloq mildly. "Did you think when my brother René died, you had seen the end of your troubles? Far from it. As you can see, we have been expecting you."

One of the thugs takes Indy's pistol and whip and tosses them aside. The others close in.

"I know you'll enjoy our hospitality," Belloq continues. "I am a terribly good host, you know."

Indy is covered. There is nothing he can do. But they must think that because you're just a kid, you're not dangerous. Nobody is paying attention to you.

"I'm getting a little sick of your charming family," says Indy. You realize he is playing for time. Is he counting on you to think of something?

Or has he got a plan?

....

If you decide to wait for Indy to act, turn to page 43.

If you decide to act yourself, turn to page 81.

Cutting through the water, coming directly toward you, are two large gray fins. You're going to be shark food!

"Did you say 'the end'?" asks Indy. "It's just the beginning."

To your amazement, he casually grabs hold of one of the fins. It turns and heads for shore, pulling him with it.

Dolphins! You grab a fin and zoom up alongside Indy.

"I thought you said 'no more playing with the fish,'" you say, laughing.

"Not fish," says Indy. "Dolphins are mammals."

Waiting for you on the beach is a search party. Indy shakes hands with his friend, the archeologist Basil Pappas. Pappas tells you why they're looking for you.

"After you two left, Costas dived to the wreck and found the missing piece of the shield," he says. "Here is the rest of the message:

(Hokk)-AIDO. IN IT, I SAW THE FATE OF THE WORLD. IN HORROR, I GROUND THE EYE TO DUST, SCATTERED IT ON THE SEA, AND (returned it to the gods)

"And you two I find playing with the fish," concludes Basil Pappas. You and Indy can only laugh.

THE END

29

To your surprise, Indy jumps into the water. "But I thought we were sticking with the raft!" you cry.

"We are," says Indy. "Just jump off and help me flip it over."

You get the idea. Once the raft has been turned over, it stops burning. Then you and Indy can hang on to it as the current sweeps you far away from the blazing island.

With a few strong kicks, you and Indy beach it on the coast a little farther north.

Later you sit dejectedly by a campfire Indy has built. "This is terrible," you mutter. "No Eye of the Fates, no Mishikani, no clues, no *anything*."

"Chin up, mate," Indy says cheerfully. He checks his waterproof holster. "Come on. We're dry enough now. Let's go."

But you don't get up. "I don't feel like going home empty-handed," you say. "And how come you're so happy? Your old friend probably just burned up on that island."

"Who said anything about going home?" says Indy, striding off into the woods. "We have a date."

"Who with?" you ask, jumping up and stumbling after him.

"With Mishi!" he says. "Now, hurry up!"

....
Turn to page 73.

Silence. What's happening? Will Indy do something?

You peer up over the seat. Indy is standing flat against the forward panel next to the partition.

He knocks. The pilot opens the partition and sticks out his gun. With a single chop of his hand, Indy disarms him.

In seconds Indy has dragged him out of his seat, handed you his gun, and taken the controls.

"Keep him covered," Indy calls over his shoulder.

You train the pistol on the Japanese pilot. He just stares calmly straight ahead, with no expression on his face.

"Don't worry," calls Indy. "He won't try anything now. He had no orders to kill us."

"How do you know?" you ask, turning toward Indy for a moment.

"Because nobody is that bad a shot!" answers Indy.

But when you turn away, the pilot opens the cargo door and bails out! You rush over and watch helplessly as his chute opens somewhere over Turkey.

"Sorry, Indy," you mutter.

"Forget it, kid," he says. "I should have taken away his parachute. Close the door. There's a slight draft."

Turn to page 86.

At that moment the coffins crumble into dust before your eyes. The old hag takes something out of her pocket.

It is the Eye of the Fates!

The light in the room grows dim. Is the torch going out? You look at Indy. He still holds the brightly burning torch, but you can barely see him.

There is only one answer.

You are going blind!

The whispering voice continues, "Welcome, welcome..."

The old woman hands the Eye to Indy. To your horror, he changes into an ugly old woman! Then everything goes dark.

You realize the terrible secret. Indy has become one of the three Fates. And so have you!

Turn to page 14.

By the time you and Indy have bound together enough birch tree trunks for a raft, it is after dark.

Very quietly, you begin to paddle out on the black water.

"Good," whispers Indy. "We've caught the Tsushima current. It'll take us right up to the island."

Drifting easily past the heavily wooded island, you see odd, flickering lights among the trees.

"Torchlights?" you ask.

"Yeah," says Indy, grabbing a passing tree limb to pull you to shore, "and they're gathered around something."

Now you can see what he means. There is a small army of men surrounding what looks like a stone casket.

One of the men holds up his torch as another begins to pry the lid off the casket.

"Any sign of Mishi?" asks Indy.

"I don't see him," you whisper.

What if these thugs get hold of the Eye? If they do, there will be no stopping them. All you can do is hope the Eye isn't in the casket.

Turn to page 76.

You and Indy quickly douse the fire and sputter into shore. No sooner have you dropped anchor than Costas jumps off the boat and runs to a small wooden boathouse at dockside.

"Hey!" you shout. "Where's he going?"

Both of you take off after Costas. You find him hiding in the dark boathouse. He is frightened. There is something wrong here, he tells you. The port is usually very busy, but now no one is around. And the explosion was a bad omen.

"Omen or not," says Indy, "whoever else is after the Eye, I'm not gonna be scared off. Now, are you coming with us or not?"

"Wh-what if the gods are angry?" stammers Costas.

"There are no old gods," you say impatiently. "They were only a myth."

"Excuse me," Costas replies, "but so was Perseus only a myth, and the Eye of the Fates. We are in danger, I tell you."

"And I tell *you* we're wasting time," says Indy, opening the door.

BLAM! Zing!

BLAM! Zing!

You are being shot at!

Turn to page 93.

Indy suddenly steers your damaged little boat into a hidden cove. You crouch behind a thicket of laurels and wait.

As night falls, the black boats cruise along the coast searching for you. But in the dark they soon give up and speed away.

"We need shelter," says Indy. "Follow me."

A full moon has risen. You set off inland on foot. Climbing over a hill, you see a small village below you in the bright moonlight.

"Where is everybody?" you wonder.

"Looks like an abandoned Turkish village," says Indy as he slips and slides down the rocky slope.

Off to the right is an old, crumbling mosque. To the left are several small stucco dwellings. Their doorways gape like open mouths in the pale moonlight.

"A ghost town," you say. "It's spooky."

"Thousands of years ago," says Indy, "the Greeks of this country worshipped Artemis, goddess of the moon. The Turks built their mosque on sacred ground."

"L-let's get back to the boat," you say nervously as Indy heads into the village.

Suddenly a thick cloud passes over the moon and you are plunged in darkness. It is so pitch black that you can see nothing.

"Indy?" you say. There is no answer. Only the sound of crumbling stones. Then a crash. Then silence.

Turn to page 121.

All you can see is white water pouring down.

The monkeys are in a frenzy. They snatch the shield of Perseus and leap over the rocks to the spruce tree at the side of the waterfall.

Indy follows them.

"Hey!" he shouts. "There's something carved into the cliff behind this tree!"

Pulling back the wet branches, you and Indy discover what the monkeys are screeching about.

Carved into the solid rock is a perfect copy of the shield of Perseus!

Now all the monkeys are pointing to the waterfall. Some of them hop under it and back out again.

Indy looks at you. "What's a little water?" he asks, plunging into the waterfall. You follow. There is a shallow cave concealed beneath the rushing water. It is as bright as day inside.

Dripping wet, you stare in awe at the brilliantly gleaming artifact fastened to the cave wall. It is a giant emerald oval, studded with rubies, staring right back at you.

The Eye of the Fates!

· ·

Turn to page 68.

"Those cliffs are too steep to climb," you complain to Indy. "We might as well have let the bees sting us to death. Besides, my ears are still buzzing."

"We don't have to climb anywhere," cries Indy, looking up. "And that buzzing is not in your ears!"

A helicopter is descending into the chasm, buzzing loudly. It lands next to the smoldering tree.

The smoke has alerted the authorities. And your father is with them.

"Whew!" says your father after hearing your story. "You're both lucky to be alive! This search for the Eye of the Fates is simply too dangerous."

You burst out laughing. "Cheer up, Dad!
What do you think the bees were guarding all
these centuries?"

"You found the Eye?" your father asks.

But Indy shakes his head sadly. He looks
at the blackened tree trunk.

"Sorry, kid," he says, "but I'm afraid we
lost it again. Permanently, this time!"

The crystal has melted in the intense heat.

But—your father's museum can claim the
shield of Perseus.

And it will be fun to tell all your friends
back in the United States just how your adventure with Indiana Jones nearly brought your
life to a horrible

END.

On the wall behind the curtain, reflecting the flickering candlelight, hang not one, but *three* Eyes!

As you and Indy gaze upon them, you realize that each has its own special power.

Glowing and pulsing in the dim light, the first one reveals everything that is happening in the world at the present moment.

The second reveals the entire history of the world.

The third reveals the future.

The things you see in them are so terrible that you look away with a shudder.

Mishi's quiet voice breaks the dreadful silence of the tomb.

"You wise man, Indiana Jones," he says. "I ask you now: What would human race do with such power?"

It takes a long time for Indy to answer. When he does, you have never heard him sound so grim.

"Destroy itself," he says flatly.

Without warning, Indy takes out his gun. Struggling against every archeologist's instinct, he fires two shots.

The loud blasts echo around the walls.

What has Indy done?

Turn to page 104.

It is Orlock. He stands on a stone ledge over the boiling sulfur, holding a golden box shaped like an eyelid.

Indy looks up calmly.

"Where should I begin?" he asks Orlock. "With the fact that you've been selling vital strategic information to various nations for huge sums of money?"

Indy holds up checks from banks in Germany, Japan, Russia, and many others.

"You can do better than that," laughs Orlock. "How do you suppose I would have such secret information? And why would these nations want to buy it from me? Come, Jones, some answers!"

"Don't worry, kid," Indy whispers to you. "He's a complete lunatic. We'll get out of this." Then he raises his voice: "I don't know, Dr. Orlock, you tell *me*."

So Orlock does, gladly. He is proud of his crimes. He tells you that he is using the Eye of the Fates to learn the secret military plans of every nation on earth. And these he sells to the highest bidders. Soon all the countries will be under his control.

How can you stop him? He's too powerful!

But Indy is frowning at the box.

"There's some part of the legend I forgot," he whispers to you, "but I can't quite—"

"There's *more*, you puny fools!" screams Kroton Orlock.

Turn to page 114.

41

You decide that the boat is the safest place to be.

In the light of the moon, you manage to find the hidden cove. But it is very dark on board the boat.

Indy doesn't answer when you call.

Have you made a mistake?

There is a creak in the deck directly behind you. It sounds like a footstep.

Before you can turn around, a heavy canvas sack is thrown over you and wrapped tightly in rope. Strong arms are carrying you down into the hold. Up on deck you can hear gruff voices.

Soon the boat is heading out to sea. You listen to the sounds around you. First a drilling sound. What is it? Then the engine stopping. Then a launch approaching. Then a launch pulling away, and silence.

Have you been set adrift? No, it's worse than that. There is sea water rising over your ankles, your knees...

They've drilled a hole in the hull! The boat is sinking...

The last thing you wonder is: Will Indy find you before

THE END?

You are sure Indy will think of a way out.

But you get very worried when Belloq has his gang blindfold you and tie your hands behind your backs.

"You are a fool, Jones," sneers Belloq. "Didn't it occur to you that there are those who would pay millions for the Eye of the Fates?"

"You have it, then?" Indy asks, stalling for time.

"Of course. A pity you will never see it," says Belloq. "In fact, neither you nor your young friend will see anything...ever again!"

"What have you done with Mishikani?" you demand, desperately trying to buy time.

"The old fool tried to fight my men at the dig site. So I brought him here. I deeply regret that he died shortly afterward. Would you like to know how?"

Your heart is pounding. Maybe you should have done something while you had the chance. It doesn't look good.

"I'll show you how," Belloq goes on. "All right, men. Ready...*aim*..."

THE END

You keep going through the narrow cave, and after a few minutes the passage widens. It looks brighter up ahead.

"Slow down," whispers Indy. "I hear voices."

Now you hear them too. As you get closer it sounds like hundreds of people singing or chanting.

"That's no language I ever heard of," says Indy, inching slowly around a bend in the cave wall.

Before you is a great hall, filled with strange-looking people. How can there be such a place deep in this cave on modern-day Crete?

The walls rise over a hundred feet on all four sides. Chiseled into the rock is an enormous sun, shooting its rays in all directions.

The chanting people are dressed in long robes. Their faces are very pale. They bow to a great stone altar. High above it, a chink in the rock permits a ray of sunlight to shine down.

There is something eerie about their loud, atonal chanting.

"Sun worshippers. In this day and age!" exclaims Indy. "I wonder how long they've been down here."

Turn to page 20.

45

Dropping out of the trees are scores of large creatures that look like small men with white fur!

"What the...!" you begin to say as they all stare at you. They look like a miniature human hunting party.

"Some kind of lost species of giant snow monkey," Indy says to you quietly. "No wonder this place is uninhabited. I don't much like them. My last experience with a monkey was no fun, believe me. They're smart. And these look dangerous."

The monkeys close in. Their eyes are wild. Their savage fangs glint in the dim sunlight. Each one is growling deep in its throat.

"There must be a hundred of them," Indy says grimly.

They are getting closer, coming from the left, the right, in front and in back.

Is this how you and Indy will end your adventure? Are you going to be torn to pieces and devoured by starving monkeys?

Turn to page 78.

46

"Go!" shouts Indy, diving through the doorway. You follow as fast as you can, zigzagging back and forth.

BLAM! Cr-r-runch!

Bullets rip into the boards at your feet and whiz past your head.

"Keep down!" shouts Indy, still running bent over, close to the dock. He fires his pistol blindly in the direction of the sniper fire.

It works. The snipers stop firing long enough for you and Indy to reach the safety of the boat and put out to sea.

You and Indy manage to repair the damage and pump water out of the hold.

"Costas stayed behind," you say to Indy.

"So we do without a guide," he says cheerfully.

But your worries are not over.

Plowing through the water are two large black cabin cruisers. And more gunfire!

As you head full steam for the open sea, you say to Indy, "Are archeologists usually so violent?"

"Persistent, yes," he replies, turning the wheel. "Violent, no. We must be up against some foreign government, or private criminals. Whoever they are, they're killers."

The swift black cruisers are just closing in on you when you sight the coast of Thrace. They'll catch up if you don't think of something fast!

Turn to page 36.

47

You and Indy arrive at the temple ruins of Delphi late at night. It is a ghostly scene. Silvery light softly outlines the huge, broken columns. In the distance the Pindus mountain range stretches placidly across the horizon.

You can imagine the spirits of ancient Greeks walking in the moonlight. The mountains look like giant gods of antiquity.

"This place is amazing," you say, turning to Indy.

But Indy is gone!

You are all alone in this temple in the middle of the night. You fight your rising panic.

"Pssst! Over here!" It's Indy's voice!

He is crouching behind the base of an old column.

"I thought I heard something," he says. "Remember, we can't be too careful. There are people who would kill us to get that Eye."

In a minute or two you hear hoofbeats. At first you imagine centaurs of mythology riding into the ruins. You know they were half man and half horse.

But then torchlights flood the ruins. It is a horde of Bulgarian brigands on horseback.

"They must have come undetected through the mountain passes," whispers Indy. "Looks like they plan on plundering Greek treasure. If they see us, we're dead."

Turn to page 117.

Slowly, terrified, the big foreigner crawls over to the trench and pulls out a silver box. Crudely engraved in the top is a picture of a human eye.

"The Eye of the Fates!" you exclaim.

The man says that he was sent by a foreign government to find the Eye. He was to frighten off intruders by dressing up as the Minotaur. The Cretan locals who attacked you were really foreign agents. When you escaped into the cave, the agents ordered him to assassinate you.

But he has failed.

You and Indy open the box. The Eye is beautifully cut out of some clear crystal substance.

It has no magic powers. That was only a myth.

"So what makes it so special?" you ask. "Why would a foreign government be willing to kill you for it?"

"Oh, there's a reason, all right," says Indy. "How big would you say this is?"

"About, um, four or five inches in diameter?" you guess.

"Which happens to make it," Indy says slowly, "the largest *diamond* in the world!"

Much later, with the assassin behind bars, you and Indy return to the salvage boat with what is truly "the find of the century."

THE END

You follow Costas's gaze up the mountain.

"Look!" you cry. Fastened to a jagged boulder high above you is the gemlike Eye. It reflects the dark clouds scudding by.

You look at Costas. He has buried his face in his hands.

Suddenly the storm breaks. It is a terrible gale. Thunder cracks like gunfire, echoing down the slope. High winds and driving rain lash at you violently.

"The curse!" screams Costas, cringing in fear. "The gods are angry!"

"Snap out of it!" shouts Indy, over a clap of thunder. "There are no gods. This is only a summer storm."

"No! No!" Costas blubbers, stumbling back down the mountain. "The Eye does not belong to us! We will die!"

In minutes he has disappeared from sight.

"Oh, great," you say to Indy. "We can't go on without our guide."

"You going to let a little thing like that stop us?" Indy asks.

Costas has made you nervous. His warning still rings in your ears.

What if he was right? If you go much farther there may be no turning back.

....

If you decide to retreat and follow Costas down the mountain, turn to page 120.

If you decide to go on, turn to page 91.

Where to start your search? Did Indy go into the stucco houses, or the mosque? Before you can decide, you see a dark spot on the ground ahead of you. It looks like a hole.

You walk over to the hole and look down. It is very deep.

"Indy!" you call. But there is no answer. Then you notice a dim light down in the hole. Could Indy have fallen down there? Perhaps he's injured! You start to climb down and notice that the hole is on a steep incline. The light leads you into a tunnel that takes you right under the mosque!

You have found the ancient ruins of the temple of Artemis! In the middle of a large underground hall is a statue of the moon goddess. Around her neck is a pendant shaped like a half moon. Some stone or jewel has been removed from it.

But the strangest thing of all is that there is a torch burning on the wall.

You're not alone in here!

Turn to page 75.

"Let it burn!" you shout, diving in and swimming for shore.

Pieces of burning branches land with hissing sounds all around you. You and Indy dive below the surface of the black water to keep from catching fire.

You swim across the Tsushima current and body surf onto the dark sand of Hokkaido's western shore.

Out of breath but safe, you look back through the mist and see the blazing inferno that used to be an island.

"I think I know what was in that casket," says Indy. He shakes his head sadly.

"Well?" you ask impatiently.

"It was Mishi," says Indy. "I'll bet on it."

"But wasn't he working with those thugs?" you exclaim.

"I don't think so," Indy says quietly. "He was a true friend to me. And to the science of archeology. He knew that the power of the Eye would be lethal in the wrong hands."

"But how—" you begin.

"Remember that scuffle above the dig site?" Indy asks. "I think Mishi was trying to get away with the Eye then. And later, on the island, he must have waited until after dark and then climbed into the casket. When they opened it, I think he ignited a bomb."

Turn to page 83.

53

Shown in the crystal is a most strange vision. You can see yourself and Indy on the mountain. But you can also see that the boulder is being struck by lightning. And that is impossible, because there *is* no lightning!

As you watch, fascinated, the Eye shows you the entire boulder breaking loose, creating a rockslide! You are seeing your own deaths— a moving picture of you and Indy buried under tons of rock.

"Can you beat that?" says Indy. "It's like a little silent movie."

"It's our fate!" you cry in dismay.

But your words are drowned out by a clap of thunder. Out of the heavy black clouds, a lightning bolt has struck the boulder, just as the Eye predicted.

You know your future looks bleak.

Turn to page 77.

Soon the passage becomes so steep that you can barely pull yourself up it. And it has become so narrow and airless that you can't breathe.

Then there is no more air.

You feel your body going limp. "Indy," you barely manage to whisper, "I don't think ...I'm...going to make it!"

You can hear Indy's voice. It sounds very faint and far away. He sounds worried about you, but you don't care anymore. You are losing consciousness!

Somewhere far away, Indy is shaking you, but you can't feel it.

As everything fades to a dark, silent blur, you close your eyes and give up.

Turn to page 6.

As you and Indy freeze in terror, the swarm sweeps around the chasm, leaving the tree bare.

And nailed to its trunk, glittering with refracted sunlight, is an oval eye made of crystal.

Carved in the trunk is one word in Greek: PERSEUS.

"Indy," you say. "There it is—"

"Shhh!" he cuts you off. "Our lives are in danger. We have to drive away the bees, or we'll never stand a chance."

He takes out his wet pistol and empties the bullets. He opens them one by one. The gunpowder is still dry. After folding the collected powder in a leaf, he begins to crawl very slowly toward the tree.

The bees are getting closer. You follow Indy, crawling as quietly as you can, to the base of the trunk.

"Do you know how to make a spark by striking flint?" he asks you.

"I think so," you say uncertainly.

Now you can feel the bees buzzing just above your head. You try to ignore them.

Indy has made a small powder trail leading to a larger pile of powder.

"Okay," he whispers. "It's up to you."

··

Turn to page 26.

They fire their rifles. But suddenly they have too many targets.

The giant crabs have burst in through the open gate of the compound!

Belloq and his thugs panic. They break up and run in all directions, shooting wildly. In the confusion you and Indy run down the empty beach. You climb into Belloq's boat.

"Nice work, kid," Indy calls to you, steering the boat into the open water. "They should be busy for a while with those crabs."

But you have made a discovery. Under a heavy canvas tarp in the stern is Dr. Mishikani, bound and gagged!

You take the gag out of his mouth.

"This time a radio will help you," he gasps. "There is one on board to call authorities!"

Much later, as you all sit calmly in Mishi's home in Tokyo, Indy pieces together what happened.

"So that Japanese pilot was your son?" Indy asks.

"Yes," says Mishi. "He now on train from Turkey, where he bail out. I sent him to keep you away. I know you not resist Belloq's trap."

"And you were so right, Mishi," Indy admits. "I fell all right. You even tried to warn me at the dig site."

Turn to page 97.

You and Indy try to persuade him, but Costas won't abandon the boat. He stays on board as you both swim for shore.

As you pull yourself up on the dock, a second explosion rips through the air.

You look back.

The boat has been completely destroyed. There is nothing left but flame and smoke on the water.

Poor Costas!

Now Indy is more determined than ever to beat your enemies to the Eye of the Fates.

"Come on," he says angrily. "We're going to see someone who may be able to help us."

About half a mile inland, you enter the grounds of a rich estate. It belongs to the world-famous historian, Dr. Kroton Orlock. He is a middle-aged Eastern European, with raven-black hair.

"So, you are Indiana Jones," he says in his thick Balkan accent. "I have heard of your quest for the Eye. Do you seek my advice? I am flattered."

Indy does not mention the attempts on your lives.

You wonder why. Doesn't he trust this Orlock?

Turn to page 103.

"That's great, Mishi," Indy says. "Lead on, old friend, lead on."

Later you are hiking deep in the wooded, snow-capped mountains of Hokkaido. The deeper into the forest you go, the wilder the country becomes.

"Archeology is a wonderful but strange occupation, is it not, Indiana Jones?" asks Mishi as you stumble into an isolated valley. "Wonderful, because friends are so willing to help. Strange because enemies are so deadly." His voice is shaking again. Is he trying to tell you something?

But Indy doesn't seem to notice.

You push your way through a tangle of fir branches.

"Yep," Indy says absently, "and luckily you're a good friend, Mishi."

You are beginning to wonder about that.

Suddenly, in the middle of this thickly wooded forest, you come upon a small clearing. There is a kind of lean-to set up over an excavation.

It is an archeological dig site!

Mishi leads you over to a tree stump. There are picks and spades lying near it.

The forest is almost too quiet.

Turn to page 94.

Dr. Orlock comes back with the drinks and sits down.

He explains that there is a legend that the Eye of the Fates once found its way to Constantinople, where it was fixed by priests to a holy icon. The icon was supposedly stolen and spirited away to Greece in the fifteenth century.

But if it is at Meteora, it will be hard to find. The monks thought of clever ways to guard their treasures.

"However," concludes Orlock smoothly, "most of the old buildings are now deserted. . . . I wish I were young enough to go with you."

The more you watch Orlock's shifty eyes,

the less you trust him. But Indy still doesn't seem to notice.

You set out for Meteora after lunch. As soon as Orlock's servants close the gate behind you, Indy says, "So, what's bothering you, kid?"

"He's either sending us on a wild-goose chase," you say, "or right into a trap. We should find out what he's up to."

"There *was* something peculiar about him," says Indy, "but I think he knows what he's talking about."

. . . .

If you decide to go on to Meteora, turn to page 63.

If you convince Indy to stay and spy on Orlock, turn to page 109.

"But we'll never get up that slope," you say. "It's too steep."

Indy uncoils the bullwhip from his shoulder. "This is longer than it looks," he says. "Stand back."

He snaps the whip straight up out of the pit. Then it falls back down. He tries two more times, until it finally holds fast.

"Got it!" shouts Indy, grinning at you. "Wrapped it around that tree trunk."

In no time you pull yourselves up and out.

Everyone is gone. The dark woods are silent.

Suddenly you hear a low moan from the bushes at the edge of the clearing. Indy runs over. Mishi lies in the underbrush. He has been struck a mortal blow.

"Forgive me, my friend," whispers the dying old man. "I tried to warn you. They force me to guide you here to get rid of you. They stop at nothing to get Eye of Fates."

Cradling the old man's head, Indy says, "Who, Mishi? Who has done this to you?"

Turn to page 116.

It is nearly sunset when you come upon the strange landscape of Meteora. Looming up from misty crevasses are massive black granite pinnacles. They form natural peaks and towers shooting hundreds of feet straight up into the air.

Perched atop some of them, you can see the corniced rooftops of the monastic buildings. They look like they were carved right out of the rock.

As you and Indy stand at the base of the tallest one, he says, "This would be a safe place to hide a treasure. No one could ever find a way up there."

"So what do we do?" you ask.

"Find a way up, naturally!" he says with a grin.

Just then, out of the mist, comes a robed monk. Indy asks him if he knows how to get to the monastery.

He doesn't answer. Is he observing a vow of silence?

Then you realize that he is deaf and mute. Using various hand signals, you and Indy try to communicate with him. He seems to be trying to tell you that the monastery has long been uninhabited. Then he leads you to an old and broken rope ladder. It only goes about halfway up the cliff. The rest of it must have rotted away.

The monk drifts off into the mist.

"Funny," says Indy. "That he came down for a stroll all by himself."

Turn to page 87.

Indy puts his arm around her.

"What's the matter, Grandma?" he asks. "Don't you know the way out?"

She breaks away furiously, hobbling over to stand between the two coffins. She points into them, the tears streaming down her face.

Suddenly there is a loud *whump*!

Behind you a gigantic stone door has rolled shut, sealing off the room! You are trapped.

"I have a terrible feeling..." says Indy.

You walk slowly across the room and peer down into the marble coffins. Inside each one is the corpse of an old woman. They look just like your weeping old guide.

"It's them," you say, half to yourself. "It's the three Fates!"

Without answering, Indy takes the torch and waves it back and forth in front of the woman's eyes. She sees nothing. You are right! She is crying for her dead sisters.

She stops crying. Then you hear a low voice.

"Welcome to the Vault of the Immortals," it says.

Turn to page 32.

The rope ladder lies flat against the sheer surface of the granite. The ancient oak slats are actually bolted in with iron spikes.

"That's safe enough," says Indy, looking up. "As far as it goes, anyway."

At first you climb carefully. The ladder is so well made that soon you are almost scampering up the side of this tall, skinny mountain.

The earth falls away below you as you reach the topmost rung of the ladder. There is still a long way to go before you can reach the monastery, which juts out over your heads above.

"Here goes," says Indy, cupping one hand around his mouth. "Hello, up there!" he shouts. "Anybody home?"

Scrape! Clatter!

You catch a glimpse of a dark robe flapping in the wind. Something is falling down the cliff at you!

Turn to page 108.

Above it, a message is etched. Indy translates it:

HERE THE EYE RESTS FOR
ETERNITY,
ITS POWER TOO GREAT FOR
MORTAL MAN.
PERSEUS.

There is a long silence after Indy reads the message. The only sound is the roar of water and the monkeys outside, still jabbering.

"Well, we found it," you finally say.

Without a word, Indy places the shield under the Eye and goes back out through the waterfall. You follow him back to the excavation site, where he takes a stick of dynamite from a box.

"Stay here," he says firmly.

From the direction of the waterfall comes a loud explosion and the sound of tons of rock falling. The monkeys take to the trees.

Much later, back at the harbor, Indy finally speaks. "You know, kid," he says, "you were wrong. We never found anything. The Eye of the Fates doesn't exist...right?"

You start up the gangplank of the boat that will take you home.

"Right" is all you say.

THE END

The abbot rises from his desk to greet you. He is a shrewd-looking man with piercing brown eyes. He is over six feet tall and broad-shouldered beneath his flowing *rassa*.

Indy introduces himself.

"We welcome scholars, Dr. Jones," the abbot says in precise English. "I trust we can be of some help. What would you like to see?"

Indy doesn't mention the Eye of the Fates. Instead, he asks to tour the grounds.

Later, while a novice guides you around the monastery, Indy asks you in a whisper, "Did you notice? The new abbot is built like a boxer! And he carries himself like a general. I thought he was going to salute us!"

Indy stops the novice at the cemetery. You notice a freshly dug grave covered with flowers, and the novice explains that the former abbot died only a week ago. Indy seems suspicious.

That night as you and Indy sit alone in your cell, he lays out a plan.

"We'll visit the abbot's office in secret tonight," he says.

Turn to page 84.

And yet, you wonder, why did it feel pain when you bit it?

Now the Minotaur has got Indy in a strange hold. It is killing him! Indy has dropped his pistol. His whip lies out of reach. He is powerless!

You pick up the flaming torch and thrust it at the beast's head. There is a *whoosh* of smoke. It is on fire!

Indy wriggles out from under it, and you both watch in amazement. The Minotaur rolls around trying to put out the flames, screaming like a human being.

Then, still screaming, it pulls off its own head!

It sprawls out on the dirt floor, coughing, and you see that it is an ordinary man.

"I give out," he says in a thick foreign accent.

You and Indy look at each other in surprise.

"You mean 'up,'" says Indy, recovering his gun. "Now what's this all about?"

Turn to page 49.

71

Trying not to splash too loudly, you swim out to the island. The closer you get, the stranger it looks. It is only about five hundred yards across. There is no sand on the beach; all you can see are masses of large, flat stones. In the middle of the island is a walled compound of some sort.

"Is it my imagination," you ask Indy, climbing out of the water, "or are these stones moving?"

"They're moving all right," says Indy, "but they aren't stones!"

The entire beach is alive with twelve-foot crabs! You'll never reach the compound alive.

Indy starts running in a zigzag fashion between the giant crabs. But they move fast. Their powerful pincers snap at his legs.

You barely manage to jump aside as one of the brutes tries to cut you in half!

Turn to page 105.

What is Indy talking about?

You follow him all the way back to the dig site. Indy lowers himself down the concealed hole and into the tunnel. He stops just outside the ancient bronze door of the tomb.

"Remember what Mishi said?" he asks you. "He said 'We meet again in the grave.'"

Indy pushes open the bronze door. Sitting in the middle of the tomb is Dr. Isamu Mishikani, sipping tea by candlelight.

"I knew you would guess clue," Mishi says quietly. "I assume your enemies are—how do you say?—'out of the picture'?"

"Mishi, you sly fox," says Indy. "What did you plant in the casket—a fire bomb?"

"You have teach me a few tricks over the years," smiles Mishi. "But now let me show you surprise I save for you."

The old Japanese puts down his teacup and rises.

You look around the tomb. Against one wall are three crypts, recessed into the hard earth. In each is the broken skeleton of a human being!

"The three women," you whisper, walking over. "The three Fates!"

But the real surprise comes when Mishi pulls back an ancient linen curtain, yellow with age.

Turn to page 40.

"What now?" you ask, trying to swim upstream.

"We don't have a choice," says Indy. "We can't fight this current. Take a deep breath, dive under, and pray!"

You pray it is a short trip to the outside world.

But it's not.

You open your eyes underwater. Ahead of you is nothing but an endless underground waterway. But above you, coming up, is some light. You tug Indy's sleeve and point. He nods.

You pull yourselves out just in time and gasp for breath. You are clinging to a tiny ledge. Your heads touch the rock ceiling. The river roars by just below your chin.

But where is the light coming from?

"Help me pull away these stones," says Indy.

You both set to work, clawing at the wall. Soon the hole is big enough for both of you to squeeze through.

You have made it to the outside!

"Now, that was a close shave," says Indy with relief. "We almost drowned."

"Maybe we should have," you say grimly.

Indy looks around. "Oh, no!" he groans.

Turn to page 8.

Someone is hiding behind the statue!

Just as you think "I wish Indy were here," out from behind the statue steps Indy.

"Oh, there you are," he says in relief. "I was getting worried."

"*You* were worried!" you exclaim. "What happened to you?"

"Simple," he says. "I thought you were right behind me when the ground caved in and I found this place. I was about to go back and look for you. I wanted to show you something."

He points to the empty pendant around the statue's neck.

"Guess what she's been wearing in her necklace for a few thousand years?" he asks you, pulling from his pocket a dazzling blue gemstone.

It is the Eye of the Fates!

THE END

The lid is off.

For a split second the gang of men simply stare into the casket. Then there is a terrific, blinding flash of light.

WHOOSH!

A strong shock wave rocks your raft. The night has turned to day. Every tree on the island is on fire. Instead of night mist, there is now billowing black smoke.

"Get down and paddle!" shouts Indy.

The explosion of dazzling flame has sent sparks into the air. Even the water around you seems to be on fire.

"Ouch!" you cry as a chunk of burning charcoal sears the back of your hand.

"The raft's on fire!" shouts Indy.

You try desperately to put out the flames. Behind you, the island is completely ablaze. The air has become as hot as an oven.

"What was that?" you ask.

"Don't think about that now," says Indy. "We're fighting a losing battle here."

Can you save the raft and get back to Hokkaido?

Should you abandon it and try to swim back?

You'd better make up your mind—fast!

....

If you decide to stay with the raft, turn to page 30.

If you decide to swim for your lives, turn to page 52.

Suddenly everything happens at once.

Indy's whip has lashed around you. You fly through the air.

Indy's arm is around you, his other hand is grasping a strong young sapling, and you are swinging down and into a shallow recess in the mountainside. You and Indy land with a thud.

Just in time.

The rockslide roars and crashes right past you.

Gradually the noise stops and the dust settles. You are safe. Indy has saved your life.

"But—but how—?" you begin.

"Don't you remember?" asks Indy. "The myth tells us the Eye has the power to see the future. But it also gave us the power to *change* the future!"

Later, back at the bottom of Mount Olympus, you and Indy stand quietly over the rubble of the rockslide. The Eye of the Fates has been destroyed forever.

As you head for home you turn to Indy.

"Do you think Costas was right?" you ask. "Were the gods cursing us?"

Indy thinks for a moment. "I don't believe in curses," he says. "But I'll pay attention to a good warning anytime it comes my way, from now on."

THE END

Suddenly you get an idea.

"Quick!" you say to Indy. "Open your knapsack." You unsnap yours and pull out two sandwiches, an apple, three candy bars, and a bag of peanuts.

"I get it!" says Indy. He pulls out his food supply and spreads everything on the shield of Perseus.

The monkeys devour the food, and luckily there is enough to go around. After they eat their fill, they seem much friendlier.

One "snow monkey," who has been licking grape jam off the shield, suddenly dances up and down, screeching. The other monkeys gather around. As soon as they see the shield, they also start screeching.

"What's up?" you wonder aloud.

Then they take Indy's hand and pull him back toward the valley!

You follow them back past the archeological dig, until you come upon a mountain stream flowing from a high waterfall. The monkeys are leaping about like furry snowballs and gesturing. They bare their teeth in grins and point to an ancient spruce tree growing next to the rock face of the cliff. What's got them so excited?

Turn to page 37.

The Eye has revealed that in the next minute, a minor earthquake will strike Delphi.

You decide to risk it.

You step boldly away from your guard. Indy looks puzzled. Is he in for a surprise!

Your guard is so stunned, he forgets to fire his rifle. You were betting on that. You walk right up to the leader in the eyepatch and raise your arms.

"Evil one!" you shout. "For this sacrilege of the temple, you will perish. The earth itself will pay you back. Earth—shake! Earth—quake!"

Nothing happens.

You're starting to sweat. They're not surprised anymore. And they're raising their rifles.

Indy must think you've gone nuts!

A few of the brigands laugh nastily. The rest aim their rifles at you and Indy.

The earthquake starts while you stand there with your arms still raised. First a low rumbling rolls across the ruins. Then the ground swells, trembles, and groans.

There is a moment of scattering in terror. In another moment all the Bulgarian men, and all the Bulgarian horses, have completely vanished into the mountains.

The Eye of the Fates is yours!

THE END

You back up slowly, edging your way toward the main gate of the compound. No one seems to notice.

"You've been stupid this time, Jones," Belloq is saying. "I forced your old friend Mishikani to lure you here. I have waited a lifetime for this opportunity."

Out of the corner of his eye, Indy has caught on to what you are doing.

"Where is the Eye of the Fates?" he asks loudly.

Belloq laughs. "There never was such a thing. It was all a hoax! A trick! My men planted that shield with the fake message. I knew you would come here as surely as a fly to flypaper."

You have almost reached the main gate.

"But you are an archeologist, like your brother," says Indy. "How could you pull such a stunt?"

Belloq laughs cruelly. "I have no reverence for your profession, Jones. I intend only to avenge my brother's death. You will die slowly—"

At that moment you throw the bolt and swing open the heavy gate. The thugs whirl around to shoot you.

Turn to page 57.

But you can still see.

"Indy," you say, "look at the walls of this tunnel. They're glowing!" You reach out to touch them.

"You'll burn yourself," says Indy. "They're hot." He stops. "I don't like the looks of this."

You peer around him. In front of you is a large open cavern. In the center is a great pit. Red steam rises from it.

Gurgle...plop!

It is a boiling sulfur pit!

But the real surprise is around to one side. By the very edge of the sizzling pit is a desk and chair. They are exact duplicates of the ones in Orlock's study! And lying on the desk, open, is the attaché case he carried from his estate.

Indy walks over to it and pulls out a cashier's check. Then another. And another.

You both stare at them in confusion. They are made out in varying amounts from $500,000 to $8,000,000! And they are paid to the order of Dr. Kroton Orlock!

He must be a billionaire!

"But I don't understand," you say. "Who's paying him all this money? And why?"

"I'm sure you've solved the mystery, Jones," calls a voice from above you. "I'd love to hear all about it!"

Turn to page 41.

"And he tried to warn us," you say, remembering Mishi's last words.

"But we didn't understand," says Indy. "It was my fault. I should have been able to save his life."

You and Indy begin to hike back to the dig site. You follow the coast until you come to the trail.

"Cheer up," you say. "Your friend would be glad to know you're safe. Besides, now we can explore the tomb. We can find the Eye of the Fates, and no one can stop us!"

Indy stops walking. "I'm afraid not, kid," he says. "If I know Mishi, there's no Eye in that tomb."

"You mean—"

"I mean it was in that casket with Mishi. It was blown up in that explosion. There's nothing more for us to do but return to Greece ...empty-handed."

So your great quest for the Eye of the Fates ends with a big zero. And with a great many questions left unanswered. Forever.

THE END

It is very late. All the monks are asleep.

You and Indy sneak past the darkened abbey and return to the cemetery.

Tombstones loom out of the wet fog that blankets the ground.

"Remember how the novice told us the funeral took place a week ago?" asks Indy in a whisper.

"Sure," you answer, "and he showed us the grave."

"Did you notice this?" asks Indy, leading you to the other side of the cemetery.

"This ground was disturbed today!" he says,

pointing to a mound of wet earth. "Somebody has been digging for buried treasure. Any ideas?"

It begins to dawn on you. The new abbot just arrived today!

"Somebody who just came from Germany," adds Indy, "and acts like a soldier instead of a priest—"

"And who knew you were coming..."

"Which means he has a radio," concludes Indy, "or else he was around when our boat blew up. Let's pay a visit to the abbey."

Turn to page 99.

Why was your pilot trying to kidnap you and Indy? Is there a conspiracy to keep you from searching for the Eye of the Fates?

"Somebody," you say thoughtfully, "doesn't want us to get to Japan."

"And somebody," answers Indy, speeding up the airplane, "is gonna be disappointed."

He is an expert pilot. You land smoothly at the airport in Japan. You are both surprised by all the Japanese press photographers waiting for you.

How did they know your plans?

An old man with thick glasses steps out of the crowd.

"Indiana Jones," he says, bowing from the waist, "we meet again."

"Mishi!" exclaims Indy.

Dr. Isamu Mishikani is an old friend and fellow archeologist. He guessed that Indiana Jones would come to seek the Eye in Hokkaido when he was listening to the radio news. Now he is offering himself as your guide to the site.

"But Hokkaido is a big place," Indy says to him. "We don't know where the site is yet."

"I have nice surprise," says Dr. Mishikani, smiling. "Very nice." But there is something wrong, you think. There is a frightened look in his eyes and a tremor in his voice.

Does Indy notice it too?

Turn to page 59.

"Hey," you cry, looking up. "I thought I just saw someone up there!"

Indy looks up, but now all you can see is the corner of the monastery hanging over the edge like a birdcage.

Was it your imagination?

"If there *is* someone up there," says Indy, "we could climb as far as this old ladder goes and then call out to him."

"On the other hand," you point out, "this ladder doesn't look very safe. Besides, maybe that monk was lying to us. It may be a trap. Why not try to find a back way up, just to be safe?"

If you decide to go up the ladder, turn to page 67.

If you decide to try a back way, turn to page 112.

You jump in, swimming hard.

But you're getting nowhere. Indy is far ahead of you. What's keeping you back?

Something's got hold of your leg.

For an instant the waves part and you see the tentacle of a large octopus tightening around your knee. It is dragging you down!

"Help!" you scream. Has Indy heard you?

Just as you are being pulled down into the swirling foam, Indy cuts the tentacle in half with his knife. The octopus releases you and slithers off, blackening the waves with its ink.

"How do you get into these things?" Indy shouts.

"Just lucky, I guess," you gasp.

With a mighty roar, the shaking islet begins to sink.

"That does it," says Indy. "No more playing with the fish. Let's swim!"

You struggle away from the sucking whirlpool just as the big rock plunges forever into the sea.

Swimming in the choppy water is exhausting. Indy starts to tow you with the whip lashed around his shoulder. But it is tough going.

"At least we're still alive," he calls cheerfully.

"Not for long!" you yell. "Look!"

Turn to page 29.

Early the next morning you arrive at the foot of Mount Olympus.

"We can't dig up the whole mountain," says Indy.

Costas says he thinks you should climb to the summit and dig there.

But you are studying the shield. There is something about the design on the front that looks familiar.

"Indy," you say, "take a look at this."

You point out that the swirling patterns resemble the general shape of the mountain. Holding it right side up, Indy can see that there is a map worked into the design!

"And look," you say, pointing to a spot marked on the western slope, about halfway up. "This looks like an X."

"X marks the spot!" exclaims Indy.

Costas agrees to guide you on the treacherous climb. But he looks worried.

After two hours of climbing you are very tired. You would like to rest. But Indy urges you on.

"Looks like a storm is coming up," he says. "We'd better hurry."

But Costas is slowing down. He is looking up the mountain.

What is he afraid of?

What has he seen?

Turn to page 50.

89

You are soaking wet. You cling to the slippery mountainside. The mighty wind seems to be trying to tear you away and send you plummeting to your death.

Inch by inch, you and Indy climb closer to the outcropping boulder. The Eye is bigger than it looked from below.

Just then, way beyond the peak of Olympus, a blot of lightning forks across the black sky. Has it been hurled by Zeus, the king of the gods?

Maybe it is not too late to change your mind. Maybe you should turn back and follow Costas back down.

Suddenly the wind dies. The rain dwindles to a trickle. There is no thunder.

"We're in luck!" says Indy, scrambling to get to the Eye. It sure seems that way. You scramble after him.

But wait.

As you look at the Eye, an odd thing happens. Very quietly, there is another flash of lightning. But it is not in the sky.

You have seen it reflected in the Eye.

Indy has frozen still. He turns to you as if to ask if you saw the same thing. But you are still watching the crystal Eye.

"Look!" you scream, almost choking with horror.

Turn to page 54.

The sun worshippers surround you. They are even more frightening up close. Their eyes are deep-set and wild. They are obviously angry that you have intruded on their religious ceremony.

The chief priest begins to shriek crazily and make stabbing motions with his knife.

You hold out your empty hands to show you are unarmed. This makes him scream louder, pointing at the altar. Now they all start screaming and pointing.

You notice that there are carvings in the wall, and they seem familiar.

"Indy, look!" you say. "The carvings on the wall look just like the design on the shield!"

Indy examines the wall. "You know, kid," he says, "this may be the break we've been looking for." He takes the shield out of his pack and holds it up so that everyone can see it.

Turn to page 4.

A sniper is trying to keep you from leaving the boathouse.

Indy turns to Costas. "I suppose the gods carry guns?" he says.

BLAM! BLAM!

There is a crash of broken glass. A window has been blown out by the gunfire.

Costas screams in terror.

"Quiet!" roars Indy. "It won't do us any good to panic. Now listen. There must be more than one sniper. I think they figure we're trapped, and all they have to do is riddle this place with bullets. There are two ways to fool them."

You could rush out the door all at once, dodging the bullets. Three moving targets aren't easy to hit. Then you could get in the boat.

Or you could duck out the back of the boathouse and head right for Mount Olympus.

Either way, you could be shot.

If you decide to run to the boat, turn to page 47.

If you decide to run to Mount Olympus, turn to page 95.

You look into the excavation from the brink of the dig. It is very deep. The bottom is lost in darkness.

"The nice surprise you were talking about," says Indy. "Is it the burial site of the three Fates?"

"You no fool, my friend," says Mishi, backing away. "I know you like get started right now looking for Eye."

As if on signal, a band of masked men dressed in black rush from the bushes! The old doctor doesn't seem surprised.

You and Indy are trapped at the edge of the pit. Both of you start swinging, but it's no use. There are too many of them. All they have to do is push!

You fall down the sharp incline, rolling over and over against dirt walls, until you hit bottom.

"It was a trap!" you say.

"Shhh!" hisses Indy. "I knew that. But the only way to find out why, was to go along with it." Then he raises his voice. "Mishi!" he cries. "How could you do this to me?"

You hear Mishi's feeble voice high above call out: "We have old saying in Japan. 'Only fool turns back on false friend.' So sorry... we meet again in grave, Indiana Jones!"

Turn to page 23.

"The shots are coming from the other side of the dock," says Indy, ducking out the back. "If we keep the boathouse between us and them, we should be able to make it to the village."

You and Costas follow, gunshot blasts going off behind you.

Just before you reach the safety of a local inn, a lucky sniper shot strikes Indy!

But he is luckier. The bullet is neatly deflected by the shield of Perseus in his pack.

Indy decides that the three of you should lie low for the night at the inn. Costas tells the innkeeper about your secret expedition. He says you are in danger from criminals who also seek the ancient artifact.

The innkeeper says you are in more danger from the gods. "They will curse you if you rob the sacred mountain," he warns you.

"It would be safer to search the ruins at Delphi," he explains. "That was also a home of the gods."

"Two homes!" you whisper to Indy. "These gods really lived it up."

But soon it will be daybreak. You have to decide where to go. There may be a curse on the mountain. And your enemies would not expect you to go to Delphi.

....

If you decide to go to Mount Olympus, turn to page 89.

If you choose to search the ruins at Delphi, turn to page 48.

95

It doesn't take long to find an underground tunnel. At one end is a passage up to the outside. At the other end is an ancient bronze door.

"That must be the tomb of the Fates," you say.

"No time to explore," says Indy. "We have to go after Mishi. We'll come back here later."

You emerge from a concealed hole in the ground just behind the dig site. The forest is deserted.

"No sign of Mishi," says Indy. "But it won't be hard to follow their trail. It leads to the coast."

It is almost sundown when you reach the Sea of Japan. In the distance, through the mist on the water, you can see what looks like an island.

"Look at these tracks in the sand," you say. "I bet they took a boat out to that island."

"We've got to follow them," says Indy. "But it's getting dark. We don't have much time. We could swim to the island, but the current may be dangerous. Or we could build a raft—but that'll take time." It's a tough decision.

If you decide to build a raft, turn to page 34.

If you decide to swim, turn to page 72.

"He tried," you say, "but we didn't understand. Remember? He said that only a fool turns his back on a false friend. But you know Mishi is no false friend. And he knows Indiana Jones is no fool."

"True," says Mishi. "And when I say we meet in grave, I try to tell you *my* life in danger too!"

"Now you tell me!" Indy laughs.

In the meantime the police have arrested Belloq and his gang. They have been sent to prison for attempted murder.

And because of the hoax, Claude Belloq has been expelled from the International Society of Archeologists.

You, your father, and Indiana Jones will soon sail for the United States. You'll be home just in time for the start of school.

Only one thing worries you. When you write "How I Spent My Summer Vacation," your teacher will never believe it!

THE END

Two of the brigands take Indy's gun and whip and guard you with their rifles; the rest finish piling up their loot. A few artifacts roll off a pile near you and land at your feet.

There is nothing you or Indy can do but wait. And you are sure they will shoot you down as they ride off. You know too much.

Time is running out.

You glance over at Indy. To your surprise, he is smiling and nodding his head toward your feet. The guards don't understand.

But you do. You look down. There at your feet, among broken water jugs, pieces of statues, and marble capitals, lies a dusty quartz globe. In the flickering torchlight you can see that it's sparkling.

In fact, tiny images are flashing and gleaming inside it, like a twinkling eye.

You are watching your own future in the Eye of the Fates! And these Bulgarians don't know it!

You see first what will happen in a few minutes, and then what will happen a few minutes later. You feel you could watch forever.

But you have already seen the answer to your problem: how to save your lives!

Turn to page 80.

The abbey is locked.

You try to look in through a darkened window. Seeing that it's made of stained glass, Indy takes out his pocket knife, carves away the lead between the colored panes, and removes them carefully.

When the opening is big enough, you both crawl through into the office.

"Breaking and entering," you say, "is illegal."

"So is blowing up boats and killing people," says Indy, lighting an oil lamp.

He begins searching the drawers of the desk and examining the books on the shelves. Not really knowing what to look for, you thumb through an old Bible on an antique stand in the corner.

"Two Bibles, one old, one new," you say.

"What was that?" asks Indy, stopping dead.

"One old, one new," you repeat. "There's a bigger, newer Bible on the desk."

"So there is," says Indy. "And it's got a nice new lock on it, too! Now, what kind of self-respecting monk *locks* his Bible at night?"

Putting his knife to work again, Indy soon pries open the lock.

You can't believe what you see inside.

Turn to page 118.

The abbot stands there calmly holding a very unholy-looking gun. It is pointed at Indy.

"You work late, Dr. Jones," he says with a smile. "But then so do I, fortunately. Did you really think I would be so stupid as to let you get away with such a pretty gem as the Eye of the Fates?"

What will Indy do now? If he goes for his pistol, the Nazi in monk's clothing will shoot him down.

"Yeah," says Indy, "how could I think you're stupid? I don't want this thing anyway. Too much responsibility. You're the ones who want to rule the world, not me. Come and get it."

The fake abbot laughs.

"An old trick, Jones," he snickers. "If you will be so good as to simply toss it to me? And gently, please."

"No problem," says Indy, about to toss the Eye.

Has Indy become a coward? Is he afraid of this Nazi?

Shouldn't you do something?

....

If you decide to lunge for the Nazi's gun, turn to page 122.

If you decide to wait and see if Indy has a plan, turn to page 17.

You and Indy continue toward the far room.

"At least we'll be able to see something in there," you say to Indy.

"Not for long," says Indy. "This is the last of the daylight."

You look into the inner room. Hanging in the middle, completely unguarded, is a large and precious-looking icon.

It is the portrait of a holy figure with a halo, praying to heaven. The icon's golden frame is inset with shimmering gems.

At its top is a pure silver oval, and at its center is a huge green emerald.

It looks exactly like an eyeball!

Turn to page 111.

You ask Dr. Orlock if he knows the legend of the Eye.

He smiles indulgently. "Naturally, my young friend, I have often wondered if it exists." He turns to Indy. "But I don't think Mount Olympus is where you should look. Have you ever heard of Meteora?"

"Sure," says Indy. "The monasteries of Meteora. What about them?"

"I believe," says the historian, "that many ancient treasures are locked away in those secret buildings. Remember, the monks who sought refuge there hundreds of years ago were also familiar with the old pagan myths."

There is something too smooth about Dr. Orlock. He may be right about the monasteries, but you get the feeling he is trying to keep you from finding something out.

"What do you think?" Indy asks you as Orlock walks off to pour drinks.

"We *could* try Meteora," you say, adding in a whisper, "but I don't trust this guy!"

Indy seems faintly surprised but says nothing.

Turn to page 60.

Two of the Eyes have exploded into a million tiny pieces. The only one remaining, the Eye of the Past, glows even brighter on the wall.

"It was the only thing to do," says Indy.

"I understand," says Mishi with a sigh.

"Well, I don't," you say.

Indy puts his gun away and goes to the Eye. He lifts it from the wall.

"Mortal man means to do good," Mishi explains to you, "but he is weak. He is tempted by evil. Give him powerful weapon and he will use it against other men. Is his nature."

Indy is looking into the Eye of the Past.

"But knowledge of the past," Mishi continues, "shows us our mistakes. This knowledge can only do good. Keep man from repeating evils of past."

As the three of you leave the tomb, you look back at the dull, shattered fragments of the ruined Eyes. Yes, you think, it was power only the gods could handle.

Besides, for all the world knows, you and Indiana Jones have found the one and only Eye of the Fates.

THE END

"You asked for it," you say. You whirl around and plant a hard kick right in the crab's mouth.

That stops it.

Jumping clear over another crab, you land next to Indy. He uses his bullwhip to drive the crabs back.

Now the crabs are getting mad.

"It's only a hundred to two," Indy yells, "but I think they're getting the upper claw!"

He's right. They have begun to crawl all over each other to get to you, their pincers snapping sharply.

You have an idea.

You jump on the back of the nearest crab. It can't reach back far enough with its pincers to touch you. Angry and frustrated, it scurries sideways. Straight for the wall.

With a laugh, Indy hops aboard another crab and comes riding after you.

"I guess this is a new species," he calls as you both reach the wall. "The *taxicrab*!"

"Bad pun," you say, vaulting over the wall. Indy springs over after you and you both land on the other side.

You are inside the compound at last.

But you have jumped into a trap!

....

Turn to page 28.

105

A newer, stronger rope ladder unwinds to just above your heads. Someone is inviting you up.

"Now, that's hospitality," Indy says. "Follow me."

At the top you are helped to your feet by a man dressed in a long black *rassa*, the monk's robe of the Greek Orthodox faith. It flaps in the wind.

"*Willkommen*," says the man in a deep voice.

He is German!

"Vee are a German order," he explains. "Vee seldom visit the vorld below."

So that's why the monastery is believed uninhabited.

"Thanks for letting us up," says Indy. "Can you take us to your, er, head monk?"

"The new abbot is expecting you," the man replies, leading the way.

The monastery is a self-contained village. There are vegetable gardens, stables for pigs and goats, a blacksmith's shed, and even a cemetery.

The monk explains that the new abbot just arrived that day. He waits for you in the abbey.

"How could he have known we were coming?" you ask Indy in a whisper. Indy only shrugs.

You enter the abbey.

. . . .

Turn to page 69.

After sunset, you sneak back on to the estate by climbing the fence. You follow Indy as he goes from window to window of the huge mansion.

There is a different person in each room! Orlock seems to be going from room to room, collecting pieces of paper.

"That's funny," says Indy. "They're all foreigners. And no two are from the same country."

You hide behind a hedge as all the guests leave, one by one, in expensive cars.

"What's Dr. Orlock up to?" you ask Indy in a whisper.

"I don't know," he says, "but that was no conference of history professors!"

The mansion is dark. After a while Orlock comes out wearing a long black cloak. He carries a small attaché case. He sets off on foot down a dark access road to Mount Olympus.

"Come on!" whispers Indy.

You follow Orlock through a grove of olive trees to the rocky base of Mount Olympus, and watch as he touches a sharp stone that juts out from the rocks.

A six-foot section of the hillside slides back. There is a secret passageway into the mountain!

Turn to page 113.

Retracing your steps, you find the tunnel. There's more light and air in this passage.

But it seems endless.

You both begin to realize you are walking through a series of interconnecting tunnels. Twisting first to the left, then to the right, they seem to lead nowhere.

"This must be an undiscovered part of the labyrinth of King Minos," says Indy. "Now we're really lost!"

He explains that King Minos once ruled Crete. He built a complicated maze from which it was impossible to escape. The king used to throw his enemies into the maze. They would be torn to pieces by the Minotaur, a giant monster, half man and half bull.

"But that was thousands of years ago," says Indy.

At that instant you hear a horrible sound. It is a deep snorting and thumping. You can't tell which tunnel it is coming from, but you'd swear it was a bull pawing the ground!

Turn to page 21.

It's the Eye of the Fates!

You were wrong about Dr. Kroton Orlock. He spoke the truth about the legendary icon from Constantinople.

You and Indy are speechless for a moment.

Then Indy asks, "When is an icon not an icon?"

"I give up," you say.

"When it's an EYE-con!" says Indy, starting into the room.

But before either of you get to the opposite wall, you realize that you weren't wrong about Orlock after all!

He has sent you into a trap. But not a human one.

You and Indy hear it at the same time. A series of noises, just as the orange sunlight disappears.

From behind you in the great hall comes a scurrying, and a flapping, and a slithering.

Poisonous spiders. A vast legion of huge bats. A sea of snakes.

These are the nightly guardians of the Eye!

You hate spiders. Indy hates snakes. Both of you hate bats. It looks like you're doomed.

But Indiana Jones always finds a way out. Doesn't he?

THE END

On the opposite side of the granite tower, you see some barely visible notches in the rock.

"Good work," says Indy. "These footholds should do the trick."

But it's a long way to the top. You decide not to look down. The closer you get, the more deserted the monastery looks.

You concentrate on climbing, pulling yourself up gradually, hand over foot. Even Indy is being careful.

You wouldn't survive a fall from this height.

Suddenly a jagged piece of the rock above you comes to life!

You almost lose your grip. The piece of black granite flies off into the darkening sky.

"Hold on!" snaps Indy. "That's what you saw before. It was just a big hawk. They roost up here."

Finally you reach the top.

The crumbling old stone monastery is empty. As the sun sets, a single beam of orange light pierces the gloom. Inside these walls, the silence is complete.

You and Indy walk slowly across the cracked stone floor and enter the big main hall. It is getting darker every second. The single beam of light breaks through into another room. You follow it.

Turn to page 102.

Orlock enters the passageway, and you and Indy follow him in, just before the wall closes. It is pitch black inside.

Indy lights a match. By the dim light you can see only the ground at your feet. Indy lights another match as you tiptoe forward. The tunnel seems to go on forever.

"This must go straight to the center of Mount Olympus," says Indy.

You just pray silently that he doesn't run out of matches.

Then you smell something very strong—almost like rotten eggs. And you hear a sound you can't identify.

Gurgle...

Pop!

Bubble...

Plop!

It's starting to get very warm.

Then Indy's last match goes out!

Turn to page 82.

"I am the greatest force the world has ever known! I shall cause the slaughter of millions in battle. I shall kill hundreds of millions by plague and famine. I shall bring destruction and despair to mankind by controlling its destiny!"

"And *I* just remembered the rest of the legend," says Indy in a whisper, taking the shield of Perseus from his knapsack.

"Now, Indiana Jones," shouts Orlock, "gaze upon the wondrous artifact you sought to possess!"

Then everything happens at once. Orlock laughs maniacally and opens the eyelid. Indy shoves the shield in front of you and says, "Look through the Eye from the back and see the future. Look into the Eye from the front and go *blind!*"

The rest of the legend.

With a ghastly shriek of terror, the madman looks into the Eye from the front, because it is reflected in the shield of Perseus. He goes totally blind and stumbles off his ledge, falling, eyelid, Eye, and all, into the burning, fiery pit!

The boiling sulfur gurgles wickedly.

"Well," you say in amazement, "I guess he's where he belongs."

"And mankind," says Indy, "has control of its own destiny again."

THE END

114

"My own people," gasps the doctor. "A power-hungry military will lead Japan into war. They want Eye because it tell futures. They will second-guess American army. Now they kill me. I know too much."

A violent cough shakes his body.

"We've got to get you to a hospital," says Indy.

"No...no, is too late," says Mishi. "But beware...must warn you now..." His eyes close.

"Warn you..." he gasps. "Monkeys..." His body slumps.

Indy stands up, removing his hat. "He's gone," he says sadly. You are both silent for a moment.

"What did he mean by 'monkeys'?" you ask.

"I don't know," says Indy, frowning. "There are no monkeys in Hokkaido. At least none that I know of."

You decide to pursue the murderers. They must not be allowed to use the Eye for their evil purposes.

But something strange happens as you start up the hill to leave the valley. The trees move as if blown by a strong wind. The branches rustle and shake. But there is no wind!

Then there is a sudden crackling and thumping all around you. What's happening?

Turn to page 46.

Hidden behind the column, you watch the thieves. They dismount and begin to dig recklessly among the ruins. They are rough and bearded brutes. They wear ammunition belts and carry heavy rifles.

"Stolen Greek Army surplus," whispers Indy.

Now the brigands are spreading canvas and piling up their loot. Statues and pottery are heaped together.

"So this is how so many artifacts are smuggled out of Greece," Indy says angrily. "They work at night and return north through the mountains."

A sharp voice comes from behind you!

There is a long rifle bayonet pointed at your neck. A huge Bulgarian forces you and Indy out into the open.

"Good idea," Indy says cheerfully. "I was feeling a little cramped."

The brigands surround you. The leader strides over. His head is swathed in a filthy bandanna, and he wears an eyepatch.

"You give no trouble," he grunts. "You not move, you not talk. Else—" He draws his dirty finger across his throat. "Yes?"

"Yes, yes!" you say hastily.

But you know they will never let you live.

....

Turn to page 98.

117

It is a phony Bible!

The hollowed-out pages are blank. Set down into the cavity is the Eye of the Fates.

It is exactly as described by legend. You know it sees the fates of everything and everyone in the world.

But you don't stop to read it like a crystal ball. There is something else in the "Bible." And this is what worries Indy.

"A communiqué from the German High Command," he says, picking it up. "So Hitler's in on this!"

These poor German monks, you think. They don't know what monstrous use their holy order is being put to. The new abbot is going to deliver the most powerful secret weapon the world has ever known—to a madman!

By tracing the actions of whole nations, the Nazis will be able to outguess and outflank them.

This holy monastery may become the center of world conquest!

"The first thing we have to do," says Indy, removing the Eye and closing the fake Bible, "is to get this Eye out of here."

"I think not," comes a voice from the open door.

Turn to page 100.

You are not even halfway down. You'll never make it to the second ladder in time.

You can only stare horrified at the vision in the Eye. You see the Nazi cut the ropes.

You see Germany start a war.

You see Germany lose the war.

But you see no sign of a future for you and Indiana Jones!

THE END

"We better go back!" you cry to Indy. "We'll never make it!"

"The storm is bound to pass!" yells Indy.

You persist and Indy finally gives in. Within the hour both of you stand at the base of the mountain.

Then, without warning, the storm ends. The sky becomes clear, blue, and placid. Suddenly you hear a whirring sound. You look up. A German helicopter hovers next to the Eye. Then German soldiers, hanging from ropes, remove the Eye from the side of the mountain. Seconds later the helicopter is gone. And so is the Eye.

You've learned your lesson. Next time you'll listen to Indiana Jones!

THE END

When the moon comes out again, you are completely alone!

You look around frantically, but Indy is nowhere to be seen.

In the distance, beyond the hills, comes the mournful howling of a wolf.

A deserted village, moon goddesses, and now a wolf! You are becoming paralyzed with fright. You open your mouth to call Indy again, but this time you have lost your voice.

Should you search for him, or return to the boat and wait?

You can't just stand here alone in the middle of the night.

If you decide to go back to the boat, turn to page 42.

If you decide to look for Indy, turn to page 51.

Before Indy can throw him the Eye, you rush the big German and grab his wrist. Maybe this will give Indy time to pull his own gun.

But it doesn't work out that way.

The Nazi is too big and powerful. His wrist doesn't even budge. And before you know it, his other arm has got you around the waist in a painful grip.

And the gun is pointed at your head.

"If you want to save your foolish little friend," he sneers, "I suggest you put the Eye back and get into that closet."

Indy has no choice, and neither have you. You spend the rest of the night locked in the closet. By the time some monks find you the next day, the "new abbot" is well on his way back to Germany. Unless there's a miracle, the Eye of the Fates will become Hitler's secret weapon!

THE END